P9-DIY-959

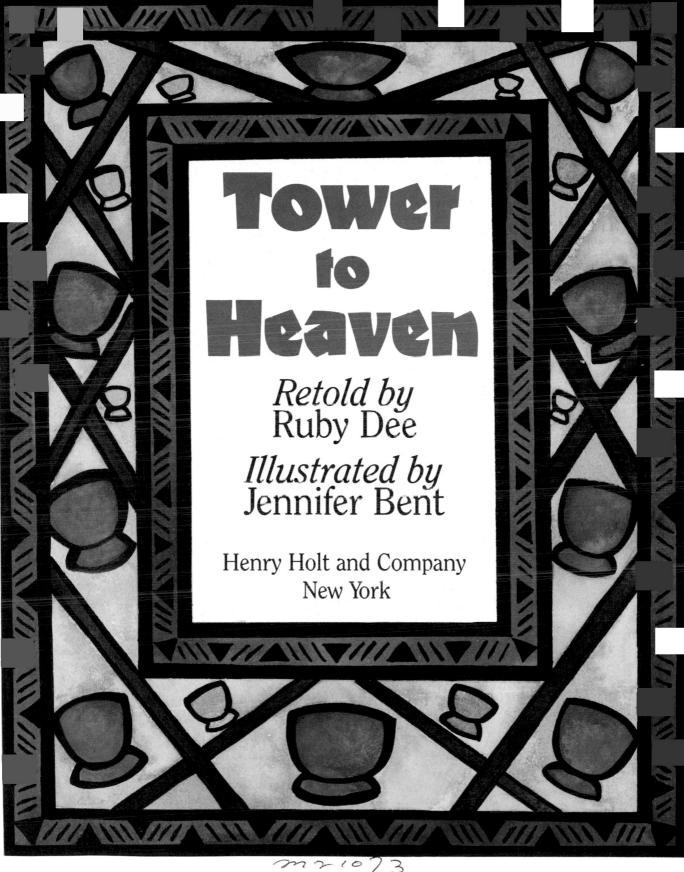

Tower to Heaven

Retold by
Ruby Dee

Illustrated by
Jennifer Bent

Henry Holt and Company
New York

mz1093
398.2
DEE

Dedicated to my grandchildren,
and to children everywhere.
With special thanks
to my daughter, Nora—
and to Ossie.   R.D.

To my mother and father   J.B.

Text copyright © 1991 by Ruby Dee
Illustrations copyright © 1991 by Jennifer Bent
First Edition
All rights reserved, including the right to reproduce
this book or portions thereof in any form.
Published by Henry Holt and Company, Inc.,
115 West 18th Street, New York, New York 10011.
Published simultaneously in Canada by Fitzhenry & Whiteside Limited,
195 Allstate Parkway, Markham, Ontario L3R 4T8.

Library of Congress Cataloging-in-Publication Data
Dee, Ruby,
   Tower to heaven / Ruby Dee ; illustrated by Jennifer Bent.
   Summary: When Yaa, who loves to talk while she works, hits the sky
god one too many times with her pestle, he disappears high up
into the heavens and the villagers decide to build a tower to heaven to
find him.
   ISBN 0-8050-1460-8
   [1. Folklore—Africa.]   I. Bent, Jennifer, ill.   II. Title.
PZ8.1.D378To   1991
398.2—dc20
[E]   90-34131

Henry Holt books are available at special discounts
for bulk purchases for sales promotions, premiums,
fund-raising, or educational use. Special editions
or book excerpts can also be created to specification.

Printed in the United States of America
on acid-free paper.

10 9 8 7 6 5 4 3 2 1

Long ago, when people needed rain for crops to grow, or gentle breezes to cool the earth when it was too hot, or medicines to heal them when they were sick, they called upon the great god of the sky, Onyankopon. Because the sky god lived near the earth, the people could talk with him every day.

That was very long ago, however. Little by little, as the people became more and more busy, they did not take the time to talk to the sky god. They let an old woman called Yaa do all their talking for them.

Yaa spoke to Onyankopon every day. As she pounded her pestle into the mortar to grind grain or mash sweet potatoes, she talked about everyone in her village, and everyone in the villages near and far. She talked so much that she didn't pay attention to what she was saying.

Once, when the earth was dry, Yaa said to Onyankopon, "You must make it rain. You want our crops to wither and die?"

That night it rained.

But the next day Yaa went back to Onyankopon and said, "When are you going to send the rain I asked for?"

"Old woman," he replied, "what is the matter with you? It rained and rained last night. It poured!"

Yaa looked at the wet ground. "Oh-ho," she said, "maybe that's why I kept slipping down in the mud. My dress is a mess!"

It's a wonder Onyankopon didn't get tired of Yaa talking so much. For many years, from sunup to sundown, everyone could hear her chatting and laughing with the sky god. Up and down, up and down, her mouth moved as she chattered away, and up and down, up and down, with both hands she would pound that pestle into the mortar.

Sometimes she got so carried away that she forgot how near the sky god was and knocked up against him with her pestle. Poor Onyankopon! He had bruises and bumps and lumps everywhere.

Onyankopon spoke to Yaa many times about the beating he was taking. Each time, she apologized and promised to be more careful. But then she would get excited and forget, and punch him with her pestle again.

Finally Onyankopon became angry and said, "Old woman, why do you keep doing this to me? If you knock me with your pestle just once more, I am going to take myself way far away up into the sky."

Yaa pleaded, "Don't go, Onyankopon! I won't hit you ever again! From this day on I will raise my pestle only this high." And she lifted it up just a little bit.

Lakeview Elementary School Library
Mahopac, New York 10541

Yaa lowered the pestle and began to speak. "Onyan-kopon, you are my good good friend. You know I would do nothing to hurt you."

She gently raised the pestle up, then brought it down again. "O great sky god," she continued, and the pestle came up a little higher, "everybody in the village loves you and thanks you for all the blessings you bring us."

She raised the pestle a little higher. "You must not ever think of leaving us," she nattered on, raising the pestle higher still. "What would we do without you?"

Yaa talked faster and faster, and higher and higher she raised the pestle, until suddenly—

"Yaa-aa-aa! Enough! Enough! That is enough!" Onyankopon screamed, for Yaa had whacked him smack in the belly. He howled with such force that it blew Yaa off her feet. By the time she recovered, Onyankopon was almost out of sight!

When the village people saw Onyankopon disappearing into the sky, they all came running. There was much noise and pleading. "Please, great sky god, come back! Come back!"

But it was too late. Onyankopon rose higher and higher, until finally he disappeared way far away into the heavens.

Soon life in the village changed. Everyone was sad, but Yaa was saddest of all. Day and night she just sat by her mortar, holding on to the long pestle. Finally her grandson Kofi tried to comfort her.

"Grandmother, you are the wisest person in the whole village," he said. "Surely you can think of a way to bring Onyankopon back."

"Bring me my thinking beads from the corner beside my sleeping mat," demanded Yaa. Kofi got them and placed them around her neck. He watched as she rubbed the beads with one hand and pointed to the top of her head with the other. She thought and thought, until suddenly—

"I know what we must do!" she proclaimed. "We will build a tower that will reach all the way up to heaven. When we want to have a conversation with Onyankopon, we can just climb up."

The people of the village cried, "Yes! Yes! We must build a tower to heaven. Why didn't *we* think of that?"

"But what can we use to build it?" asked Nikai, Yaa's son.

"We can use stones," suggested the chief.

"Too heavy," said Bumi, the fisherman.

"How about yams?" asked Olu, the farmer.

"Too mushy," said Afia, his wife.

The people argued among themselves about what would be best. Finally Yaa raised her pestle and said, "We will build our tower with mortars. Let us collect them all and take them to the top of the tallest mountain!"

"We'll help too, Grandmother," said Shika, the youngest of Yaa's grandchildren.

"Yes!" said the village chief. *"Everyone* must gather mortars."

The people looked high and low. All the mortars they could find in their village, and all they could find throughout the valley, they piled on the top of the mountain. The tower grew higher and higher, until at last it reached the heavens.

"Eh-eh-hooray!" exclaimed all the villagers as they sang and danced. "We have built our tower to heaven! From now on each of us must take time every day to talk to the sky god. No more will we depend on Yaa to speak for us!"

But Yaa hobbled ahead of the villagers and was the first one to climb the tower. As soon as she got to the top, she called out, "Onyankopon!" But he did not answer. Again she cried, "Onyankopon, I have found you!" But from the sky came only silence. "Why won't he answer me?" she wondered out loud. "He can't hear me," she decided. "I'm not close enough.

"We must make the tower higher!" Yaa yelled down to the villagers below. "We need one more mortar. I know I could reach him if I had one more mortar."

"One more mortar! One more mortar!" The cry went down the mountain and throughout the land. Everyone searched, but none could be found.

"We've brought all we could find!" came the cry from below. "Shall we go to the far country for more?"

"No! No! There is no time!" shouted Yaa. "My head is full of things to tell the sky god. I must talk with Onyankopon *today*! Just take one mortar from the bottom of the tower and get it up here as fast as you can."

Everyone pushed and pulled to remove the bottom mortar so they could pass it up the tower to Yaa. When at last they plucked it out, for a moment the tower hung in midair!

But before the old woman could put the mortar on top and call "Onyankopon!"—KERTHUNK! The tower dropped back to earth and began to sway.

"Help! Help! Save me, Onyankopon!" she cried. The people below ran back and forth with their arms outstretched, hoping to catch her if she fell. But Yaa hung on. When the tower stopped swaying, Yaa saw that she was no higher than she had been before.

"Send one more mortar up from the bottom!" she shouted.

"One more mortar! One more mortar!" Again the people pulled the bottom one free and sent it up to the top. And as before—KERTHUNK! The tower sank, and swayed back and forth. Seven times Yaa called for the bottom mortar, and seven times the tower was exactly one mortar short.

"Grandmother," called Shika, "if we keep taking out the bottom mortar and putting it on top, the tower will never get taller. If it is ever to reach Onyankopon, we must find *another* mortar."

The people of the village turned to one another and whispered, "That's a very good idea. Why didn't we think of that sooner?

"One more mortar! We must find one more mortar!" they all chanted as they scattered far and wide.

Nikai called up the tower, "Don't worry, Mother. You will speak with Onyankopon soon. Hold on!"

But Yaa was calling so loudly to Onyankopon that she did not hear Nikai or see the people of the village going off in search of one more mortar.

Even now the search continues. And it is said that on days when the air is very clear, you can see Yaa still standing on top of the tower. She calls out to Onyankopon, and even though he does not answer, she tells him about the people in the village, about their joys and sorrows, about her hopes and dreams. And from time to time she shouts over her shoulder. "One more mortar! One more mortar! All we need is one more mortar!"